ISBN-13: 978-0615460444 (Fred Landerman)

ISBN-10: 0615460445

Printed in the United States of America.

# PANAMA RED

## A COLLECTION OF "SEA" STORIES

By

**Fred E. Landerman**

These are tales of the many exploits of a sailor in the U. S. Navy during the Viet Nam Era conflict. Some are true, others only partly true, having been "borrowed" from tales told to me while serving aboard the USS Topeka.

Any resemblance between the characters in these stories and any living person is coincidental and unintentional, with the exception of Pope Paul the Sixth. It was my pleasure to meet him on my twenty-first birthday and tour the Vatican Museum.

# DEDICATION

This collection of short stories is dedicated to the men and women who served in the military during the Viet Nam Era conflict. So many of them came home to a different political climate that held them in disdain for their service to their country. They were called 'baby-killers', spit on and reviled in the media and in public. They went to a foreign and extremely dangerous place to be wounded or killed and upon their return they found no haven or peace.

May those who have given their lives so that the citizens of these United States may enjoy their many freedoms never be forgotten. They gave, some willingly and some were drafted, so that future generations may never have to pay that same price.

"Old men start wars, but young men have to fight them and end up paying the price." Unknown

# FOREWORD

Sea stories are those tales that are told when sailors don't have much to do and a lot of time to do it. The better the story, the more listeners there are, and often the story is retold with a few embellishments, until it gets to its 'perfect' state.

Because of the competitive nature of the male gender, these storytellers would attempt to outdo the others with their credibility often in jeopardy. To give credence to the story, they often include a cousin, friend, or uncle who was supposedly there when the story took place, or they have some authority figure who will swear to its truthfulness.

One thing to keep in mind while reading is that these are not 'fairy tales' and should not be treated as such. A 'fairy tale' begins "Once upon a time…", while a 'sea story' begins with "Now this is no bullshit..".

PANAMA RED, Table of Contents

viii

# PANAMA RED

## CHAPTER ONE – The Big Idea

He stared at the handcuffs on his wrists. It seemed almost unreal that this was happening to him, although he had thought about it from time to time. He had known all along that sooner or later they were bound to catch up with him. Three kilos is a lot of grass, even on a big ship like a cruiser.

It had started out as a joke between a couple of guys in the commissary division, talking about how they could enjoy the cruise across the Atlantic and in the Mediterranean with a few bags of grass. Eddie knew nothing would come of it; it was just normal sailor BS. But his mind was working on an angle that might get some weed aboard if he could find the right connection when they pulled into Panama City.

Eddie was in charge of the refrigerated spaces on board the USS Topeka, and as such had to go with the commissary officer when he went to purchase provisions. Most of the time he was just along for extra labor in case the lieutenant needed boxes moved, or if he had some items he wanted carried back to the ship. That day didn't seem any different than before until they got to the market place. There he began to 'feel' an opportunity coming his way.

He watched as the lieutenant made his way through the market looking at the different fruit on display. He hung back a little, hoping to talk to a vendor he had seen who seemed a little too aggressive when they had passed by. As the lieutenant marched along making comment on this vendor or that, Eddie stopped in front of the man and picked up a banana.

"Quantos?" he asked. "How much?"

"For you senor, it is free, a gift."

"How much is it if I want three kilos?" Eddie asked.

"I'm sorry senor, but I don't understand, "the man replied.

Eddie smiled. "I'm looking for some grass to help pass the time on a long voyage, but I guess I was wrong. I thought you might be able to supply such a thing."

"Oh no, amigo. There are some friends of mine who might be able to help you, but I do not conduct such a business.  It was told to me some time ago that only certain men may make transactions such as you mention. Perhaps if you were to come to the Tres Pajaros Cantina tonight then these men might talk to you."

Eddie turned and walked away, quickly catching up with the lieutenant.

"What were you doing back there?" he was asked.

"Just trying out my high school Spanish," he replied. "It's a lot different than in a classroom. They talk much faster than I thought."

. . . . .

Eddie was nervous when he entered the cantina. It wasn't near the usual sailor bars, and it looked a little run-down. He didn't see any other sailors inside as he made his way to the bar.

"Una cervesa, por favor" he asked.

"What kind of beer you want?" the bartender replied, watching Eddie.

"I'll have a San Miguel and a glass please," Eddie answered.

The bartender served him his beer and went down to other end of the bar, talking to a young girl who looked as if she were the local whore.

As he sat there, Eddie thought to himself, "This is crazy. You could get killed in here and no one would know. "He almost got up to leave, and then thought better of it.

He sipped his beer slowly, waiting for some kind of sign that the men he was looking for were there. It seemed like hours had passed since he walked in but it was only a few minutes.

The girl kept glancing at him from time to time, obviously trying to flirt with him. He kept his face turned but only far enough so he could still see her in the mirror. After a while she walked over to where he was sitting and stood in front of him, her intentions far too obvious.

"You want to have a good time?" she asked.

Eddie looked her over and could tell she wasn't more than fifteen or sixteen at the most. By the look on her face, she had been doing this for some time now.

"Not tonight, maybe tomorrow," he said. "I'm waiting to talk to some men."

"Maybe they don't come here to talk to you. Maybe you should go now."

"No, I will talk to these men if they are here. I want to buy something from them."

"Cuidado amigo, these men you are waiting for are very bad. They may just kill a little one like you and take your money."

"Then they wouldn't get much money tonight. I don't even have enough to pay for a fine girl like you if I wanted to," and he laughed.

"For you it would not be so much money," she smiled. "And Maria would be very good to you."

"Maybe tomorrow night pretty one, not tonight. Tonight I must talk to these men."

She strutted back down to her seat at the end of the bar, satisfied that she had done her best. Eddie just smiled and went back to his beer.

The vendor from the market entered and crossed the room, "Senor, it is good to see you again. I have told my friends and they will come soon to discuss this matter."

Eddie ordered two more beers, making sure to come up with just enough money to pay for them. He didn't want Maria to think he had lied.

"What is it going to cost me for three kilos?" Eddie asked.

"That will be up to my amigos, senor. Now we shall wait and they will come. Then we talk of money."

They sat in silence sipping beer as the minutes ticked by. Eddie watched as the bartender polished glass after glass, mesmerized by the monotony of the routine, listening to the radio. The songs on the radio were about love and betrayal and broken hearts from the few phrases that he heard and understood.

An hour later, the door opened and two men entered. Eddie noticed a feeling of danger as they made their way to one of the side tables and sat down. Both of them wore suits, and looked as if they belonged in a board room instead of the little cantina. He glanced at Maria and could see fear in her face. The bartender was standing absolutely still, as if he too was afraid to move.

"Are these your friends?" he asked the vendor.

"Si, senor. They are the ones I spoke of."

"Will you introduce me to them, then?"

"Si, senor. But be very careful, they are bad men. If they don't like you, they may kill you."

"So I've been told," he said.

As they made their way to the other table, Eddie noticed the bulges under the coats of each man. He wondered if he should just walk away, but he kept going toward them like a moth to a candle.

The vendor spoke to them quickly in Spanish, too fast for Eddie to understand what was said. The closest one looked up at Eddie and smiled.

"I understand you want to buy something from me."

"Three kilos," Eddie replied flatly, trying to keep from showing his nervousness.

"Did you bring the money?"

"Not tonight. Tonight I came to talk with you about price and how it can be delivered."

"Do you have the money close by?"

"No. The money is still on board the ship, and it will stay there until you have delivered the three kilos and then you will be paid."

"You are very careful for a young man. But it is not permitted for me to go aboard the ship as you already must know."

Eddie smiled. "Then perhaps we can exchange the money on the docks next to the ship, once the marijuana is delivered."

"How are we to deliver this thing on to your ship when there are guards watching everyone come and go?"

"That part will be easy," Eddie replied. "The lieutenant who was with me today purchased several boxes of fruit. If you were to place some of the marijuana in each of the boxes instead of the regular packing, the sailors will carry it on board for you and no one will know."

"Perhaps. But if they find out, then I will have no marijuana and no money."

Eddie stood there for a moment. That was something he hadn't thought about. His mind raced with thoughts on how to convince them to do this. After a moment it came to him.

"We both are taking risks, amigo. I am taking a risk that you will even deliver the stuff, and you are taking a risk that you will get paid. Besides, you haven't even told me what the price is."

"Three thousand dollars," the man replied.

"I'll pay two thousand and no more."

"You would be advised to not argue with me, senor. It is worth much more than the price I am asking."

"Maybe so, but I want to make some money too, my friend. I will pay two thousand four hundred."

The man smiled, "You are much too young to be so serious. For you, I will sell it at two thousand seven hundred."

"Well," Eddie scratched his head. "If we are to do business, I will pay two thousand five hundred. It must delivered tomorrow as I said and I will meet you by the docks."

"Bueno, we are agreed. Now we will leave you. Take Maria and have a good time, she is my gift to you for tonight."

At the mention of her name, Maria was soon by his side and together they ordered shots of tequila. The bartender was very prompt in getting the drinks poured and in refilling Eddie's glass, even when he said "no mas" or no more.

# PANAMA RED

## CHAPTER TWO – Business as Usual

The next morning Eddie was sick like never before. The night with Maria had been more than he had expected. She kept her promise to be "very good" to him. The liquor and Maria had just about made him be late getting back to the ship. He had been drunk before, but not like this. Between the hangover and the fear of being caught smuggling the grass onboard, he was a wreck.

He watched the whole loading operation from the deck, about ready to climb out of his skin. Had someone touched his arm, he probably would have jumped overboard. Surprisingly, the whole thing went just like he said it would. The boxes of fruit were stored neatly away, just waiting for him to ration out to the galley. If anyone had noticed that the boxes had grass in them they didn't say anything.

He made his way to the docks and almost passed up his contact. He looked up and down the pier and didn't see the man he'd done business with. He was about to go back aboard when someone touched his arm. The man who last night had been so neatly dressed now looked like a poor migrant worker.

"You have something for me?" he asked politely.

Eddie didn't reply, just bent over as if to tie his shoe and slipped an envelope under a stack of pallets. He straightened up and walked on down the pier and waited while the man retrieved the envelope. After a moment, the man walked by and whispered as he passed, "Buena suerte, amigo."

Eddie waited until the ship had left the Caribbean and was well underway across the Atlantic before he rolled his first joint. It was better than he had expected, the rush almost immediate. He pulled in another lungful and held it. He knew he could get double or triple the price of the crap they sold in San Diego.

He was sitting at the aft end of the "Oh-Two" level and just watching the ocean passing by. There was no moon and the stars seemed so close he could reach out and touch them. The ship's wake was visible for quite a distance behind due to the efflorescence of the plankton dying when the propellers had churned through the water. Damn, he thought to himself, this shit is really good. He finished the joint and wandered back to his bunk and some deep sleep.

His night with Maria was a gift from the man he had done business with, but Maria had given him a gift also. About a week after leaving Panama, he began having a burning sensation when he pissed. One day later he was standing in line for sick bay waiting to get looked at by the corpsman.

"You've got the clap," the corpsman said, laughing. "Looks like you'll be seeing me twice a day for the next two weeks."

Eddie thought the corpsman enjoyed his work a little too much, the way he jabbed the needle in his butt. He also thought the corpsman was a fag, but nobody could prove anything. It didn't matter to Eddie; it wasn't any of his business what someone else did.

His first sale was to Danny, the New Yorker who had jokingly started the whole thing. He casually mentioned that if he had some grass, would Danny buy it.

"Hell yes I'd buy it, but there ain't any around here. Even if there were, it's probably crap."

Eddie produced a joint and said, "Try this. If you like it, I've got some for sale."

The first kilo was sold before the ship reached Naples. Eddie was right about the price. He was getting twenty five dollars for what would have been a nickel bag in the states. He was careful who he was selling to, only four or five people had bought from him. What they did with it or who they sold it to didn't matter to him. He'd already made his money back and doubled it. He hadn't spent much money on himself, just an occasional night on the beach at a really good restaurant. With the money from the grass and the money he'd made making "payday" loans he had several thousand in cash.

The "payday" loan was probably the best money he'd ever made and the easiest. He could loan ten dollars today and get back fourteen on payday. As long he didn't write the names and numbers down, they couldn't do anything to him. Besides, he wasn't forcing anyone to make the loans. They knew what they were doing.

He laughed at some of the guys that borrowed money from him, they were so stupid. All they had to do was stay on board ship for a night or two and they would still have some money in their pockets. Instead they spent all their money on liquor and whores with nothing to show for it.

There were a couple of guys he wouldn't loan money to no matter what. He had seen them with their wives when the ship pulled into dock before they started this cruise, and he didn't want to be responsible for screwing up a family that needed all the money they could get. It was hard enough raising kids on the small amount the sailors were paid. He'd come from a large family and knew how important it was to be able to count on a steady income. Several of the guys had tried to borrow money from him, but if he knew they were married he wouldn't loan them any amount no matter the reason.

Eddie had begun hanging around with the Chaplain's assistant, a guy named Ray, a short skinny Mexican from Ventura. He liked to go to museums and art galleries and then to a nice restaurant. Eddie didn't like the museums so much, but he really liked the restaurants. When he was young, the meals all had a certain monotony to them. They consisted of Hamburger Helper and variations of any kind of casserole his mother could use up leftovers in. He had wanted to be a commisaryman or cook from the time his older brother Bob had told him that on board ship cooks were treated better than most.

The Navy was noted for having good food and on board the Topeka it was true. The Topeka was runner-up nearly every year for four years for the Ney Award for best large mess afloat. The captain really wanted to bag that trophy and to help get it he'd recruited a young chef-in-training that he was acquainted with from Boston. Charlie was definitely a great cook and he knew it. Most of the time his attitude was obnoxious and the rest of the time it was unbearable. In spite of himself, he was a pretty good teacher on cooking. He made it a point to pass along at least one tip each day.

When Eddie and Ray went to a restaurant it wasn't hard for them to spend a hundred dollars for their meal. They made it a goal to try a new dish each time they went out. As the meal was served they ask about the appetizer if it was one they hadn't had before, or the entrée. Their server wasn't thrilled with having to stop and explain each item as it took up his time. They were usually 'forgiven' when the waiter found out the size of the tip. After that, they were best friends. Often they would order an after dinner drink and just sit there enjoying the surroundings and doing the one thing Eddie liked the most, people watching. Most of the time Eddie ended up picking up the tab. It seemed like Ray was always forgetting to bring enough money for dinner.

He kept a small log or diary of the places they had eaten and what the dinner was. He had it in the back of his mind to maybe someday open up his own restaurant.

# PANAMA RED

**Chapter Three** – The Russians


After Naples they were supposed to be headed to Greece, but that didn't happen right away because of the Israelis and the Egyptians getting into a short term war. The Topeka was assigned to patrol along the coast of Israel near the Israeli/Egyptian border for nearly a week. The only interruption in the monotony was when a Russian destroyer decided to start cutting back and forth across the bow of the Topeka.


The destroyer would keep crossing back and forth each time coming closer and closer. The skipper tolerated this routine for a couple of hours, and then he got tired of playing with them. He sounded General Quarters and everyone scrambled to their stations. The captain began pointing the big guns at the bridge of the destroyer and tracking them back and forth to follow their movements. This lasted for about an hour then the Russians apparently didn't like this game of "chicken" and left the area. The Topeka went back to normal watch and resumed the patrol as before.


The only other time the Russians were seen was the next day when they flew one of their bombers past the Topeka at a low level. That time the skipper knew they were coming and had the missiles mounted and tracking before they even got there. When they saw the missiles locked on they left rather abruptly. Eddie admired the captain. He had been up to captain's mast before and knew that the captain was firm but fair.

Instead of going to Athens, the Topeka was told to return to port in Naples. When they arrived, the Russian destroyer was tied along the same dock that Topeka was assigned to, but the harbor master apparently like Americans better so the Topeka got the leeward side where the wind didn't push the ship against the pier.

Prior to being released to go on liberty the Captain made an announcement that the Russian sailors were likely to be encountered while the crew was ashore and that under no circumstances were they to confront them. He made it very clear that any enlisted man or officer that didn't conduct themselves with proper behavior would be severely disciplined.

Eddie listened carefully to what the Captain had to say and then went his way toward the outskirts of Naples where there was a circus or carnival that had set up. Eddie liked the taste of the Italian Chianti and that is what he usually ordered when in a tavern. In a restaurant he might ask the waiter to help him select a wine to go with the entrée and thus learn what he liked and didn't like.

Eddie made his way to a little outdoor tavern that served good Chianti where he and a couple of other sailors had been before.  When he and his friends arrived they found their "usual" table occupied by some Russian sailors. In spite of some grumbling, he convinced his friends to take a nearby table. None of his group was what you would call hard drinkers.  Most of the time it was beer or wine and maybe an occasional shot. They sat and made themselves comfortable and ordered a round of drinks. Because he was curious, Eddie asked the tavern keeper if he could buy a round for the Russians. Of course he could, why was there a doubt?

When the tavern keeper served the Russians and explained who had paid for them there was silence and stares. Apparently they weren't used to having their 'enemy' buy them drinks and they weren't sure what they should do. Eddie asked his buddies to stand and raise their glasses in a toast to the "flat-hats" meaning the Russians. They did as he asked and when they raised their glasses and then drank, there was an instant buzz from the other table. If any sailor in his group did understand Russian, it wouldn't have mattered. They were talking fast and interrupting each other constantly.

Just to have some fun Eddie asked if any of his group spoke Spanish other than himself and Ray. Nobody raised their hand so he and Ray began talking loudly in Spanish. One of the flat-hats spoke a word or two trying to get Ray's attention. Ray turned and asked him a question and it seemed like forever before he answered. Before he talked to Ray he questioned his own group in Spanish, but Ray whispered in Eddie's ear that the sailor was afraid of being turned in as a spy.

When they finally started talking, the flat-hats would listen attentively as Pyotr, the translator, would tell them what Ray said. This back and forth went on for some time and the tavern keeper was very diligent in keeping the glasses filled. This form of top-level peace talks was profitable and he certainly didn't want to spoil the mood.

One of the Russians ordered shots of vodka, but when the tavern keeper showed them the brand he was instantly shouted down. Pyotr explained that there was one brand they preferred over everything else and they had been served that when they first arrived. The tavern keeper explained that he had run out of that brand and couldn't leave to get more. Eddie asked how much for two bottles and was told forty dollars. He gave the tavern keeper a fifty and told him to send someone to get two bottles. The errand boy was back within ten minutes and the peace talks resumed.

When the sailors and the flat-hats stumbled their way back to the pier and there they split up saying their good-byes. Eddie was written up for being out of uniform because he didn't have his scarf or hat, but he was wearing a flat-hat that he'd traded them for. He was confined to the ship for the remainder of the time they were in port, which was good for him and his lending business. It was during that time that he was approached by one of the sailors who had recently been transferred aboard for some grass. He swore up and down that he normally got his weed from one of the people that bought from Eddie, but Eddie wasn't sure of this guy and didn't tell him anything about grass or even whether he knew who this sailor was talking about.

In a surprising twist of fate, when Eddie went to Captain's mast for being out of uniform, he was told he wouldn't be doing any time looking for the Golden Rivet. The term Golden Rivet refers to cleaning the bilges, those spaces below the deck grating in the engine rooms. Besides the usual oil and water mess is the added joy of the engineers using the bilges to pee in instead of climbing two ladders to the heads. Sometimes if the engineers knew who was coming they might add a floater or two to the mix. All in all, cleaning bilges was a very unpleasant experience and one Eddie was happy to miss out on.

Eddie was so surprised that he forgot protocol and asked why he wasn't being punished. The Captain obliged him by pulling out a letter and reading him part of it. "To the Captain of the American cruiser; I want you to know that some of your sailors displayed a courtesy I would not have believed possible by Americans if it weren't for the fact that my nephew was the one who made me aware of this. My nephew Pyotr told me that two sailors were especially kind in buying drinks and even sending for his favorite brand of vodka, sailor Eddie and sailor Ray. Relay my thanks to them for their kindness to my nephew and his friends."

# PANAMA RED

## Chapter Four – It Had to End Sometime

They were back underway and only a few hours out of port when Eddie was approached by the same sailor as before trying to buy some grass. Again he told the guy that he didn't know what he was talking about and went about his daily duties. A few hours later the sailor that had been buying from him before came and wanted to get some grass. Eddie was pissed off that this man had told the other sailor who he got his grass from and so he told the man he'd sold out. He said he'd have find another source for weed if there were any on board, and then he went back to work.

Eddie kept having this funny feeling that something bad was about to happen and that he should be careful. He told his other customers that he was out of grass and didn't know when he'd score some more. He kept it shut down for the whole time they were at sea, thinking that maybe after Athens he would sell to a couple of guys that he thought he could trust.

Athens was just like the post cards. The port of Piraeus wasn't anything like a post card. Eddie did his usual routine of accompanying the lieutenant when buying fresh produce, but this time it was at the Air Force base. There was no haggling or arguing with the vendors, just how much do you want and when do you want it delivered. It took them all of two hours including the driving time. After he got back on board, he spent the rest of the day making up the next two weeks menus based on the fresh produce they had purchased.

That night Eddie had dinner by himself at a very nice restaurant near the Acropolis. Ray was with the Chaplain at some function on the Air Base. He looked over the menu carefully, not sure what he should try. He asked the waiter for a suggestion and he recommended the roast leg of lamb with roasted herb potatoes and baby carrots with fennel in a honey herb sauce. Although he wasn't used to eating lamb, he tried it and was really astonished at how good it was.

His mother had cooked some "lamb" for him and his brothers when he was young and it ended up tasting like old wool socks. Since then he'd always been afraid of anything labeled lamb. Maybe it was the shot of ouzo he ordered with the appetizer that gave him the courage. Anyway, the lamb and the vegetables were really good as was the pistachio sorbet, and the after dinner cognac was the perfect end.

Eddie almost fell asleep on the taxi ride back to Piraeus. Had he fallen asleep, it could have been disastrous. Some cabbies had been kidnapping sailors, demanding ransom, and then if the ransom were not met within a couple of hours, the sailors would be found with their throats cut. Having seen some of the slums of Piraeus he could understand why someone might choose that way to make a living.

They stayed in Athens for five days, apparently awaiting a part for one of the turbines on the ship. Eddie didn't mind much, it was a great place to eat. He tried some more Greek food and also some Turkish food. Between the two, he preferred the Greek. He also did some shopping at the stores, buying a solid gold initial ring and a couple of gold chains. He visited the Parthenon and the Acropolis, just like the rest of the tourists.

Two days after they left Athens, they came to the dry storage space where Eddie was working. The master-at arms and the sailor who'd tried to buy grass from him ordered him to open the different spaces until they found what they wanted. They loaded it all into a couple of large cardboard boxes and had Eddie accompany them to the master-at arms office. It was there that they interrogated him for nearly four hours. Eddie didn't answer any questions and instead kept repeating that under the

Uniform Code of Military Justice he was entitled to legal representation. They finally gave up and stopped asking questions.

Eddie wasn't sure what to do, but he knew he didn't want some JAG rookie to represent him in something this important. He asked if he was going to be able to call an attorney to represent him and they laughed at him. He calculated in his head how much money he had in the Credit Union and knew it was over twenty thousand. It just might be enough to keep him in the Navy.

They put him in the brig to await captain's mast. He just sat there for quite a while until a stray thought crossed his mind and he started chuckling to himself. He was thinking how nice it would be to have a little something to help pass the time.

# SHAKE DOWN CRUISE

**Chapter One** – A Night on the Town

The Topeka had been in dry-dock for several weeks getting retrofitted with new bottom plates on the hull and repairs to the port shaftway. The repairs were required because of the previous Captain's misjudgment on throwing a concussion grenade that slid along the hull and was sucked into the shaftway by the propellers. The seam that was opened when the grenade exploded caused an immediate flooding of certain dry goods storage spaces and a call to General Quarters. To say that the Captain was embarrassed was an understatement. His peers heard about the incident and he became the butt of several jokes in addition to earning the nick-name of "Bang-Bang".

While all the repairs were being done, most sailors took the opportunity to go on leave, if they had any coming, and visit their families. Eddie didn't have any leave built up having just gotten out of boot camp, so he just stayed on board. He was assigned to the deck division even though he'd put in for commissary division. The thought of swabbing decks and scraping paint for four years wasn't appealing, so each day he'd stop by the commissary office and ask if there were any openings. Each day he got the same answer and was told to check back in a day or two.

At night there wasn't much to do for those on board, maybe a chess game or reading a book. Eddie went from one compartment to another looking for new reading material. He was bored and just about any type of book would do to fill the time. He'd learned speed reading when he was very young, his parents being teachers. His mother had taught each of her children the alphabet when they were only two. By the time they were three they could read basic books and the newspaper.

Where they grew up there was no television, so reading was their form of entertainment. Fortunately there was a Bookmobile of sorts that came twice a week, so they had an endless supply of books.

Payday finally came around which meant he could afford to go to the Fisherman's Wharf to one of the nicer restaurants and have a nice meal. That was his intention to start with, but he got sidetracked by a couple of his friends. They wanted him to show them a few of the notorious places that San Francisco was famous for. Eddie knew of one place, Finnochio's. He also knew what kind of 'show' that was put on there and in a sudden burst of inspiration, he told his buddies of this "great place" they could go to. He chuckled in anticipation at the thought of his buddies cuddling up to some of these 'girls'.

Together they managed to catch the right bus and soon were in the downtown area a few blocks from their target. Eddie warned the others of a 'cover charge' that they had to pay because this place had so many women compared to the number of men and that he didn't have enough to pay that and still have money for dinner later. They agreed to pay his fee for him so he could join them. They were soon inside and seated at a table, but Eddie said he'd prefer to sit at the bar. He claimed he wanted to be faithful to his girlfriend even though no such person existed.

The group of sailors was soon approached by a bevy of young 'women' and drinks were ordered. Eddie watched carefully and saw the concern on the sailor's faces when they went to pay for the first round. He'd been warned of the "drinks" the 'girls' were ordering by an older brother who had experienced this same treatment a few years prior. The Champagne Cocktail was actually lemon-lime soda with a splash of white wine and it was expensive. The more of these drinks the 'girls' were able to get the customer to order the more money they made at the end of the night.

After the second round of drinks, Eddie motioned the bartender and asked him if he would tell the girls to take it easy on the Champagne Cocktails. The bartender was not inclined to stop such a well-paying routine and said so. Eddie politely informed him that three of the four were underage and the Shore Patrol was right outside the door. Before either one of them could say anything more one the sailors jumped up, yelling"She's a He! I mean she's a guy! Holy crap!"

It seemed that Lester Hayworth had been using his right hand to do some exploring and was upset at what he'd found. Young Lester was a football player from Nebraska and his previous sojourns with his wandering hands on willing cheerleaders had never encountered a package like he'd just found. His sudden outburst brought a cacophony of jeers, catcalls, and laughter. The sailors sitting with him apparently realized that the 'girls' they'd been fondling were not girls after all and they too had sheepish looks on their now red faces.

Eddie turned back to the bartender and smiled. "Looks like the party's over now, anyway. It's been fun."

The bartender looked at him and said, "you knew what kind of place this was when came in, didn't you? Yet you let your buddies sit down with the ladies anyway? You're some kind of bastard, kid."

"Yeah, I guess I am at that," Eddie said.

# SHAKE DOWN CRUISE

**Chapter Two** – Cruising the Farollons

Hunter's Point dry-docks are located on the south side of San Francisco and away from the winds that batter the West Coast on a regular basis. San Francisco Bay is most of the time quite calm and pleasant to cruise on in a sailboat. Once a ship leaves the safety of the bay, it becomes quite obvious why so many of the trees and shrubs are slanted. They grow that way because of the constant wind. The winds are especially fierce around a small group of islands known as the Farollons, where many of the ship's captains test their vessels with a "shakedown cruise."

Eddie was ready for anything. He'd heard from his brother that 'sea-sickness' is something you never get over. You have it or you don't is what he'd been told. Because he'd never had any kind of motion sickness before, Eddie wasn't sure what to expect. He'd also been told that it takes some time to develop your 'sea-legs', being the ability to walk at an angle and adjust to the rolling of the ship.

Because of his constant questioning about being transferred to the commissary division, the First

Class Petty Officer of his deck division had Eddie assigned as a mess cook. He was still part of the deck division, but reported to the galley to do clean-up work, pot scrubbing, or whatever they might need.

He did every chore given him with more enthusiasm than he would have normally in an attempt to have the commissary officer notice him. When his two week tour as mess cook was complete, he traded with the bosun's mate that was supposed to take his place.

He was at his usual chore of swabbing down the mess deck when they left the safety of the bay. He immediately noticed because of the more prominent side to side rolls that the ship took. His bucket and squeegee went rolling to the other side of the ship, then rolled right back. He caught it with the mop and locked down the wheels. One of the cooks mumbled something about having the bucket too full, but Eddie was too late to remedy the situation. At the next roll, the swab bucket tipped and spilled its contents onto the deck endangering anyone attempting to pass through the mess deck. It took a combination of luck and skill to go from one end of the mess deck to the other without falling or sliding into one of the tables.

Eddie quickly realized that he had to get it cleaned up before someone got hurt and he was blamed for it. The cook who was watching tossed him a couple of terry cloth hand towels and some string. He told Eddie to tie the towels to the bottom of his shoes and he wouldn't slide so much. The trick worked, but didn't help with the volume of fluid that was being 'artfully' arranged on the floor by some of those who had just eaten breakfast. He kept mopping as fast as he could, but was barely able to keep the walkways clear of fluid.

The captain was putting the ship through all kinds of maneuvers and changes in speed. Eddie learned later that the captains liked the currents off the Farollons because they would put more stress on a ship's hull than nearly any other place except near Tierra del Fuego. That would be a little too far to call for a tow back to port if something broke down.

Eddie worked until late that evening keeping the mess deck clean and passable. Apparently somebody had noticed his work, because the Chief Petty Officer came out and told him to stand down; his watch was over and had been for an hour. The Chief asked him his name and Eddie told him. He also told the Chief that he had been trying to get transferred into the commissary division. The Chief just grunted and said he'd check into it. He made his way back to the deck division and grabbed a quick shower before climbing into his bunk.

It seemed like he'd just gotten to sleep when they shined the light in his eyes. He knew better than to complain about being awakened so early, the next time they came would be worse. He climbed out of his bunk and was quickly dressed and headed for the galley. He liked it there early in the morning, especially when the coffee urns had just finished perking. There were four urns in a row and they started with one and got it brewing. They then filled the others and started them brewing before the first was empty. If the sailors didn't get their coffee first thing in the morning, things could get nasty. This morning wasn't bad, most of the sailors were still trying to get their sea-legs back and were tired from the previous day.

Eddie was assigned to peel potatoes, which wasn't as dreary a chore as it may sound. The potato peeler was a rotary device that 'sanded' the peelings away from the potato, but it required constant watching or the entire batch could be peeled away to nothing. Eddie didn't like wasting food, so he would stop the peeler when it had just removed the skin. That meant more manual labor for him to remove any of the defects and the eyes, but for him it was worth it. He had noticed that the menu never had baked potatoes on it and asked why. He was told they were too much trouble and none of the cooks liked doing them.

He finished peeling all the potatoes and delivered them to the galley and asked what else he could do. The two cooks were there talking with the Chief and all three stopped and stared. Apparently none of the other mess cooks had asked for more work and this was a first for them. The one cook who had talked to him the day before told him to swab down the mess deck. The other mess cook hadn't kept up with the job very well due to a bout of seasickness. Eddie just smiled and said sure and went to it. He knew he was making points with the Chief by doing whatever they asked.

When he finished the mess deck, he changed the water in his swab bucket and started down the starboard passageway in front of the galley. He completed that and did the port passage in back of the galley. When he finished the two passageways he went back to the mess deck and was just in time to clean up after a couple of new recruits that had chosen that spot to create "deck art" by losing their breakfast. He hated cleaning up puke, but it had to be done so he just did it.

It was almost lunchtime so he put away the swab bucket and cleaned himself up. As he was sitting on the head, he heard the other mess cook telling his buddy what a chump Eddie was to do all that work. He was bragging about telling the cook that he was seasick so he didn't have to work. Eddie just listened and waited until after they'd left and then went to get his lunch. As he ate, he thought about what they'd said and wondered if maybe they were right. He'd signed up for commisaryman on the advice of his older brother who'd gotten out of the Navy a year before. He was told that the cooks had some crazy long hours when they worked, but they only worked seven days out of fourteen. He also knew that there were three ratings that nobody messed with, cooks, paymasters, and personnelmen. Cooks could literally starve you, paymasters could hold up your pay for months, and personnelmen could have you transferred to the South Pole.

He was sitting and holding his tray while trying to eat when an older petty officer handed him a half slice of bread and showed him how to place it under the tray to keep it from sliding as the ship rolled from side to side. He also said the bake shop didn't like it if you wasted bread, so only use a half slice at the most.

He was about finished for the day when the cook told him the Chief wanted to see him. When he got the mess office, the Chief and an officer were talking so he waited. The Chief noticed him and motioned him to come in the office and close the door. He looked at Eddie and then introduced him to Lt. Harris, the mess officer. He then told Eddie that he had asked to have him transferred to the commissary division. Eddie smiled and said thank you and backed out of the office.

# DIFFERENT PORTS, DIFFERENT PEOPLE

**Chapter One** – Acapulco and Puerto Vallarta

When he heard that the Topeka would be stopping in Acapulco, Eddie was excited. When he was growing up and also when he was working in the orchards with the migrant workers, he'd heard that Acapulco was such a wonderful resort to visit. But he'd also been warned that it wasn't cheap to visit there, prices for everything were almost the same as in El Norte. He'd been taught to never judge anything until he'd experienced it for himself, so he went ashore with an open mind.

One of the first stops he made was to a small restaurant on the not-so-well-traveled side street that was away from the glitzy hotels. Compared to the hotel area, this area might even be considered a slum or ghetto. He knew from talking to the migrant workers that the standards of living in Mexico were lower than the States. His view of the area was that overall it was fairly clean and well kept, although the houses were not very big or highly decorated. Some had the exteriors painted, but others didn't.

As he entered the restaurant, he noticed a heavy woman behind the bar putting bottles of beer in the cooler on the back wall. She didn't bother to turn around, just asked. "Que quieres?"

"I'd like a cold beer, please. Do you have Tecate or Dos Equis beer?"

She spun around quickly and looked. "Yes senor, we have both. Which one do you want?"

"Dos Equis, please. And are you still serving lunch?"

"Yes sir, what would you like for lunch? We have tamales, tacos, enchiladas, arroz con pollo, or would you like a menu. I'm sorry it is written in Spanish, we don't get many Americanos in our neighborhood."

"May I see the menu, please? I took Spanish in school, but I can't understand most of the people here because they talk so fast and I don't get all the words."

She handed him the menu and went back to filling the cooler. When she was done, she handed him a cold beer and a clean glass. "Did you find something you want?"

"I think so," he said. "Is this enchilada del mar a seafood enchilada, and if so what kind of seafood is in it?"

"It has shrimp, fish, and crab meat in it and a sauce on top. Would you like some beans and rice to go with that?"

"Yes please. I must say you speak very good English. Where did you learn?"

"When my family worked in California picking fruit, I learned to speak it. My father didn't learn very well, but he tried hard. I helped translate for my parents because I was the oldest."

"Where about in California did you work? When I was younger I picked fruit too. Mostly prunes around Marysville and Yuba City."

She smiled and said, "We stayed in the Richland Housing in Yuba City when we worked there. We usually picked peaches, but sometimes we picked pears for Dana Packing. Only once or twice did we pick prunes."

"I know where Richland Housing is, we lived just six blocks from there. A lot of the kids that stayed year round in Richland went to school with me."

She turned and started to go into the kitchen and then stopped. "I have some salsa and chips if you'd like."

He nodded yes and she got a small bowl of salsa and a large bowl of tortilla chips that had to be homemade. She then went into the kitchen and he could hear her humming along with the rattling noises from the pans as she prepared his lunch.

He was silent the whole time he was eating lunch, he didn't want to stop. The enchiladas were very good and the beans weren't like the usual refried beans that were served in other places. They were pinto beans cooked with some peppers and onions and some type of meat. Spicy, but not really hot, they had an excellent taste. Eddie normally didn't like beans, having eaten too many servings of them when growing up. His mother had never been one to add any spice or flavor to her food, although she did try from time to time. His parents were teachers and didn't make a lot of money. The idea of having steak was unheard of until he was much older.

When he finished eating, he sat back and sipped the rest of his beer. He was almost full and the only thing that would make him full was something sweet. He asked if she had any desserts.

She brought out a tray with some cookies and a small cup of what looked like vanilla pudding. "I also have some fresh fruit that I could slice for you, if you'd like. I have bananas, papayas, mangoes, melon, and oranges."

"I'd like some papaya and mangoes with a squeeze of lime juice on top, please," he said.

She left and then returned shortly with the fruit. He ate slowly, savoring every bite. When they were at sea, they rarely got any fresh fruit. He wanted to enjoy this while he could. After he finished, he asked how much he owed for the meal and she told him sixty pesos. He almost choked, but got out his wallet and was reaching for some twenties when she laughed and said five dollars American. He pulled out a ten and gave it her. She returned with change and he smiled and folded her hand closed over the money.

"Thank you for a very nice lunch and a nice conversation. I really enjoyed it here," he said.

"When I get back home and drive by the Richland Housing, I'll think of you."

He walked out and began making his way back to the ship. He was in a very good mood and even the whores grabbing at him didn't change that. He walked past the vendors and didn't even bother to look at their wares; most of it was tourist crap anyway.

Three days later and they were in Puerto Vallarta. He agreed to stay on board for another sailor and serve his watch in the galley, for a price of course. When the sailor came back aboard and asked if he could 'borrow' the twenty he'd paid Eddie, Eddie said sure for the regular payday loan rate. It occurred to him that he might not see the guy again, unless he was there when he got paid. Thank goodness the paymaster always set up two tables in the mess deck; it would be easy for Eddie to spot the guy coming through the pay line.

Between Puerto Vallarta and Panama City there was a payday and Eddie made sure he was in the galley when they started paying. The sailor was on the port watch in the galley and Eddie on the starboard watch, so they rarely had contact with each other. Today that was about to change. Eddie was in the back of the galley by the ovens when the other sailor tried to slide through without being noticed. Eddie went out the other door and around to the mess deck just in time to be next to the sailor when he signed the paymaster's book. Eddie just smiled and held out his hand. It was to be the start of a new career.

Because he'd been on watch the entire time they were ported in Puerto Vallarta, Eddie asked some of the others what it was like. Some said it was a bust, the beer was warm and the women cold, while others said just the opposite. He noticed that the guys that talked about their exploits with the women were usually lying their ass off, so he would listen politely and then be on his way. Because of his being alone, some of the other cooks thought he might be a queer. Eddie didn't bother to comment one way or the other.

# DIFFERENT PORTS, DIFFERENT PEOPLE

**Chapter Two** – Panama Canal, Guantanamo Bay, San Juan

After a short stop in Panama City, the Topeka went through the Canal and all the locks. It was a slow process, but very interesting because of the guide who was on board and describing the different parts of the Canal and the history of its construction. Eddie was assigned to the bake shop that day and it was miserably humid. They had every fan they could find blowing to keep the shop clear enough to see. Harris was in charge of the shop and somehow had scrounged enough dry towels so they weren't constantly swimming in their own sweat. They were on their third sixty pound run of dough for bread when the guard for the Admiral yelled attention on deck. Harris didn't even bother to look up, thinking it was someone pulling a prank. He nearly jumped out of his skin when the Admiral tapped on his shoulder and asked if he could help.

Surprisingly the Admiral was very good at handling the dough. He said he and his wife loved to bake when he was home and had the time. Eddie felt sorry for the Marine who was standing at the door. He offered the man a towel but the only response he got was a quick shake of the head indicating "no". Eddie just draped the towel over the

Marines shoulder and went back to work. Handling hot bread pans on a hot day isn't fun, even when the Admiral helps.

Eddie pulled the bread pans from the ovens and dumped the fresh loaves on the counter. He then put them one by one on the cooling racks prior to slicing. The yeasty smell of fresh-baked bread was something he knew he'd never tire of. He noticed the Admiral also breathing deeply, taking in that distinctive odor. Harris motioned to Eddie to go to the galley and get butter. They often cut into a fresh loaf and covered it with butter and ate while it was still warm. When Eddie returned, they did that very thing and it wasn't until the Admiral invited him to help himself that the Marine actually moved. He quickly wiped his head down with the towel and then got a large slice of hot buttered bread. They sat there in the humid bake shop looking like a bunch of wilted daisies, eating fresh bread with butter.

When the Admiral left, he thanked them both for letting him help. He said that he'd rather be here in the bake shop working with them than up on the bridge listening to a bunch of junior officers attempting to kiss his ass. Eddie tried not to laugh, but wasn't successful. The Admiral just patted him on the shoulder and said it was okay and thanks for trying to help Lance Corporal Carver.

A few days later the Topeka pulled into Guantanamo Bay and dropped anchor. Nobody knew for sure why they were stopping here as they weren't allowed to go on the base, but there were more than enough rumors to go around. The bosun's mates had lowered the Admiral's barge and the Captain's barge and they said there were some prisoners taken from the brig on the Topeka. Another rumor was that the Topeka was to be the transport for some "civilians" that had come on board and were being hidden away in the officer's quarters. Eddie thought the whole thing was being speculated about way too much, which is what happens when sailors have too much time to think. The only thing Eddie cared about was that there was another payday between Gitmo and San Juan. He'd been letting people know discreetly that he had money to loan. He realized the risk he was taking by loaning money, the Navy called it usury and he could be jailed or even dishonorably discharged. But the advice from his brother was paying big dividends. If there was no written record of who owed what, then they couldn't charge him with anything.

San Juan was about like going to Florida, only farther south. Everything was either in Spanish or English so anyone could understand. They were to be in port for four days, so Eddie went ashore the first day to see what he wanted. After that, he stayed on board and made himself available to those who might want to borrow money. By the time they left port, he'd loaned out over four hundred dollars. When the next payday came, he planned to be at the end of the pay line with his hand out.

There was one small flaw in the plan that Eddie hadn't counted on. Two of the sailors he'd loaned money to had orders to be transferred to another ship and would be transferred in Mayport, Florida when they took on stores. He didn't know about them transferring until the next payday which took place prior to them passing through the Straits of Gibraltar. He kept looking for them and finally asked one of the personnelmen that he knew. The loss wasn't as much as it could have been, but it still hurt. He asked the personnelman if he could arrange to get information on anyone transferring out soon, so it couldn't happen again. He'd lost one hundred twelve dollars of his money, but still made a profit of forty eight dollars. He gave the personnelman a twenty and told him to give him a list of transferees before they hit the next port.

There was one part of San Juan that Eddie didn't like. It had to do with a souvenir that someone decided to keep. A beautiful Spanish Helmet conch had been found by one the sailors swimming in the clear blue water around San Juan. He brought it up to the surface and got it on board, but had no clue what to do with it, unaware that the conch was still in the shell. He showed it to one of the cooks who said he knew just what to do. Joe was a Guamanian that had enlisted right after they started building steel ships, or so it seemed. Eddie had tried several times to pronounce Joe's real first and last name, but wasn't able to. It looked like someone had taken a Scrabble set and dumped out the letters and then blindfolded had picked so many for his first name and a different number for his last.

Joe had taken a clothes hanger and hooked the conch with it and hung it upside down so the weight of the shell would pull the animal out of the shell. When they had accomplished their task, Joe and the sailor took the conch to the galley and prepared it. They used it to make a conch stew, which they shared with Eddie and several of the other cooks. It was delicious and tasted similar to the abalone that Eddie used to dive and get off the coast of Northern California.

There was a side effect to the conch that none of the cooks were happy about. Joe hadn't told the young sailor how to take care of the shell and so he'd stuck it in a corner under the bottom bunk below Eddie. At first the three guys that slept in that tier of bunks didn't say anything, not sure of what the smell was. The next night they weren't so polite to each other and accused each other of the nastiest farts on record, each pointing at the other two. The worse the smell became, the louder and nastier the comments until someone actually bothered to look under the bottom bunk. Because it was wrapped in a T-shirt, it wasn't recognizable for what it really was. They pulled it out and unwrapped it which sent a plume of malodorous stench throughout the entire compartment.

The evil shell was rewrapped in the T-shirt and then in a garbage bag and thrown overboard despite the loud protests of the sailor it belonged to. It took nearly a week before the smell was completely gone. During that time there were comments made by some of the crew that they didn't understand why some of the cooks were spending so much time at the mess decks.

# DIFFERENT PORTS, DIFFERENT PEOPLE

**Chapter Three** – Palma Mallorca, Spain

The Topeka passed through the Straits of Gibraltar and headed for Rota, Spain to the naval base there for replenishment of provisions. The day before they got to Rota, one of the engineers asked Eddie to loan him two hundred dollars. The engineer wasn't aware of Eddie's talk with the personnelman and didn't understand when Eddie said no. He looked at the engineer and noticed a very nice watch on his wrist. Eddie offered the man forty dollars for the watch, but was promptly refused.

After three weeks at sea, not including the stop at Rota, the Topeka pulled into port at Palma Mallorca. Palma Mallorca is an island south of Spain and a major tourist destination, especially from the northern European countries. It was also the cruelest punishment that the Captain could have inflicted on his crew. All of the beaches were 'clothing optional' and so this crew of sailors began to invade them. Most of the older sailors didn't understand what all the fuss was about, while many of the younger sailors just couldn't stop staring. Like anything else in life, you can get used to just about anything, so Eddie gave up the beach scene and opted for a cantina where he heard someone playing a classical Flamenco guitar.

The interior of the cantina was dark. It took Eddie almost a minute before he could see any of the back walls. The person playing the guitar was sitting on a stool and playing as if there were an audience of hundreds. Looking around, Eddie saw three couples sitting at the tiny tables and one lone man at the bar. He sat at a table and was asked right away if he wanted something to drink. He asked for a glass of wine and was served a red wine that was very robust. It tasted good and he realized he hadn't eaten since the night before. He asked the waitress if he could get some snacks. At first she didn't understand and left to ask someone what he meant. She then vanished into the back and came out a few minutes later with a plate of what looked like hors'douvres. There were three of each of the four different items.

He asked what they were and was told tapas. Nothing else, just tapas. They all tasted good so he didn't ask what was in them. The tapas and the wine made him feel comfortable, but he didn't care. There didn't seem to be much he should be on guard about in this little place. He was sitting there enjoying the music when the waitress sat down next to him at his table. He was slightly surprised, but not alarmed.

"You come on the big American ship?" she asked.

He had his mouth full of tapas when she asked him, so he just nodded yes.

"Where you from in America? Where you live?"

He finished eating and then answered, "I'm from California, and I live in the northern part near San Francisco."

When he said California her face started to light up, but when he said the northern part she seemed disappointed.

"You ever see movie star? They live in Hollywood in south. You ever go there?"

"Yes, I've met some movie stars, and yes I've been to Hollywood twice. I've met George Kennedy and Jim Brown when they made a movie near my house."

"So you know movie stars. You introduce me if I come to America?"

"I said I've met them, we're not friends. Now, can I have another glass of wine?"

"Oh, yes of course. I'll be right back."

He noticed when she left that she stopped and whispered something to the guitarist. It must have been about where he was from, because the guitarist began strumming a rendition of "I Left My

Heart in San Francisco". The guitarist was very talented, playing a twelve string guitar so well that it sounded like two different guitars playing. Eddie was impressed by his talent and when the song was finished, he applauded and then asked the waitress to give the guitarist the five he'd pulled from his pocket. She took the five to the musician, but on her way was chattering in Spanish about how he'd only played one song and received a big gratuity while she waits on the Americano and has yet to receive anything. At least that's what Eddie thought she said. His high school Spanish was unable to keep up with her rapid-fire speech.

The wine was good and the music was good, but it was time to go so Eddie asked the waitress how much for the tapas and wine. When she told him, he deliberately overpaid her by ten dollars and told her it was for the great service she'd provided. She giggled and kissed him on the cheek. He wondered if he'd tipped her a twenty would she have followed him out the door.

The one place Eddie did want to see before dark was the Cathedral. It was a magnificent building of stone built in the twelfth or thirteenth century. The stained glass windows were impressive as were the various figures carved into the stone. What impressed Eddie the most was the size of the stone block used in the construction. Having worked with his uncles on a few construction projects putting up block walls, he knew how strenuous it could be. But working with stone blocks that weighed nearly a ton and a half was something he could only wonder about. How they placed those huge blocks in the arches that high was something he could only speculate about.

When he stepped into the church from outside, he could feel the temperature was lower by several degrees. He asked one of the priests how it was cooled, but he didn't answer, just pointed to another priest.

Eddie asked the second priest how it was so cool inside when outside it was so warm. The priest only spoke Spanish, Castilian Spanish at that so it was hard for Eddie to understand him, but he found out by short sentences and lots of gesturing that the heat was pulled out of the Cathedral by its natural tendency to rise. As the heat rose and exited via some small windows at the top of the main chamber, it pulled cool air from the basement into the room. Eddie learned it was something the Moors had been using for centuries in their buildings and the architect who designed the Cathedral adapted its use. Eddie also learned that the first priest wasn't being rude; he'd taken a vow of silence for a year.

He wandered around the city for a while, stopping at a few vendor stalls and looking at the different things for sale. He bought a set of castanets as a souvenir, but wasn't really interested in much else. He slowly made his way back to the pier and finally onto the ship. He had watch in the morning, so he ate as soon as they opened for the evening meal. After dinner he played a game of chess with Ray, the Chaplain's assistant. He never won because he was always trying aggressive moves, but he was learning something each time they played.

He was in his bunk about to sleep when someone grabbed his arm and shook him. As was his normal reaction, he came up swinging. The person jumped back just far enough to avoid being hit.

"Hey man, I heard you loan money. I need a hundred right away. I'm in a poker game and they raised and if I don't call, I'll lose everything. Can I get the hundred right now?"

The person talking was one of the guys who worked in the engine room. He was big, red-headed, and smelled like he hadn't had a shower in a month.

"No. The bank's closed tonight. Come see me tomorrow if you still need the money." Eddie could see the anger building in the man's face, and wished he weren't lying down and vulnerable.

"Come on man, I won't need the money tomorrow. I need it right now. I'll pay double the normal rate if I can get it now."

Eddie had this feeling in the bottom of his stomach that he was going to regret doing this, but he said, "Okay, get out of here and I'll meet you on the mess deck with the hundred."

After the engineer left, Eddie grabbed a hundred out of his locker and stopped by Ray's compartment and asked him to come with him. When they got to the mess deck, Eddie made the engineer state the terms again. When the guy had finished, Eddie handed him the hundred and told him to never come to his bunk again.

The engineer just laughed and said, "Yeah man, whatever you say." He walked away with the money in hand, back to his 'game'.

The following day Eddie was serving food on the mess line when the engineer came through. Eddie smiled and asked how the game had come out, trying to be polite. The engineer just shook his head and continued on through the line without answering.

Eddie stayed on board the remainder of the time they were in Palma, standing his watch and one for another of the cooks who had fallen 'in love' with a German tourist. She must have had expensive tastes, because the cook not only paid Eddie to stand his watch, but borrowed a hundred dollars. It seemed as if it were going to be a very rich payday for Eddie.

The next stop for the Topeka was to be in Malta, but not before some fleet exercises that would take three weeks. Eddie was standing at the end of the pay line on payday. All of the guys who owed him money paid him except the engineer. The red-headed engineer just looked at him and asked, "What do you want?"

Eddie quietly said, "The money you owe me, remember?"

"That's too bad. I need all the money I got so I can send it home. I guess you're just outa luck."

Eddie knew better than to make a noise on the mess deck with the paymaster close by. If the engineer decided to spill the beans on Eddie's payday loans, he could be put in the brig and court-martialed. Eddie just smiled at the guy and said, "We'll play it your way then."

He knew where the engineer worked and where he went to take a shit. He waited until the right time, and then with the wringer handle from the mop bucket, he kicked open the door to the toilet stall and hit the engineer in the head four times. He held out his hand and when the engineer shook his head no, he hit him again. This time when he held out his hand the engineer gave him his wallet. Eddie took out the exact amount the guy owed and then another twenty.

"That's for making me have to come get my money," he said and threw the wallet back at the engineer. "For your sake, you better tell everyone you banged your head in the engine room."

# DIFFERENT PORTS, DIFFERENT PEOPLE

**Chapter Four** – Malta and Naples

Malta is an island in the southern part of the Mediterranean, just off the coast of Africa. It was once the gateway to Africa for the Italian merchants wanting to trade with the Arabic tribes. After the Second World War, Britain had established a military base on the island, but not much else had been done since then. Eddie listened to the other sailors as they returned to the ship and quickly decided that he didn't need to go ashore to 'experience' Malta.

Since he'd had to collect his money the 'hard way' from the engineer, he'd had fewer sailors coming to him for loans. He still had some regular customers, the kind of guys that just can't control how they spend their money. He often wondered if they'd ever had to handle money before they enlisted. Some of them had absolutely no sense when it came to money. One guy came to him the night before payday to borrow twenty so he could send it to his girlfriend 'right away'. Eddie didn't bother to explain to him that the envelope would sit in a mail sack until they hit port again. He didn't think it would make any difference.

He ended up going ashore with the commissary officer to help pick out some fresh fruit. The vendors they were to see had set up outside the main gate of the British base, so when they were done the new ensign suggested they go have a beer. Eddie reminded him that it wasn't proper for the officers to be seen with the enlisted and that he didn't feel like drinking. He sat at a small café outside the main gate while the ensign went to the Officer's Club to get a cold one. The café had a variety of coffee drinks and some tea drinks and a few fruit drinks. He asked what the fruit drinks were made of and when told that one had mango juice and tea, he had to try it. The combination was very sweet and strong. He finished three by the time the ensign returned.

Apparently the ensign wasn't aware that European beers are higher in alcohol content than the American versions. He'd had six tall beers and was feeling no pain when he saw Eddie. Together, they made their way back to the launch and Eddie sat with him until he started 'chumming' the ocean. When he'd finished he sat back and went to sleep. When they arrived at the Topeka, Eddie called for some help, explaining that the ensign was too enthusiastic about his job. Eddie told them that Ensign Sorrel had insisted on eating some of each of the fruit they'd bought to make sure it was good. He swore that the Ensign had only had one beer, so he didn't think it could be the beer. He hated to see the guy get written up for "conduct unbecoming of an officer". After all, he'd just gotten the job of Commissary Officer.

Two days later, the ensign called Eddie into his office and thanked him for covering for him. He was changing Eddie's assignment to be in charge of the storage spaces and provisions on the ship. He said there would be quite a bit of recordkeeping involved, but he'd seen Eddie's test scores when he enlisted and knew he was very good in math. He also told Eddie that he only had to answer to the Chief and himself and that his watch was weekdays only in port. His hours were from five a.m. to two-thirty p.m.

He took over the duties of the storage spaces and when he saw the records, he nearly quit. Weaver, the Petty Officer who'd had the job prior didn't keep any records. They didn't have a clue as to what the inventory was supposed to be. One thing they had an abundance of was dehydrated sliced potatoes, as well as dehydrated shredded potatoes. Eddie had rarely seen hash browns on the breakfast menu or au gratin potatoes on the dinner menu so he would definitely mention it to the Chief. He also found a big supply of spices and herbs in the dry storage area, but the expiration dates on the boxes were four and five years old. He thought about just ordering everything that was out of date, but then got the idea that the one man who could tell him what to order would be Charlie, the chef.

Charlie was less than enthusiastic about ordering spices and herbs. He said the senior cooks had come down on him hard for even suggesting they change up the menu or they add a couple spices to a dish to liven it up. Eddie did his best sales job and finally talked him into a basic list that they could start filtering into the menu if they could get the Chiefs help. Charlie was instantly curious and wanted to know how. Eddie suggested that Charlie accompany him to the dry storage spaces to see what was there.

One the first things to catch Charlie's eye was the stack of sliced potatoes, the second was the two cases of canned dried grated Parmesan Cheese.

"I know a recipe that will use both of these and the sailors will definitely come back for seconds," Charlie said.

"You probably have dozens of recipes like that Charlie, but it won't do any good unless the good ol' boy cooks get told by the Chief to try them."

"Yeah and just how do we do that? The Chief is glued to the list of Navy recipes that he was given ten years ago and just won't change."

"He will if it's HIS new recipe. If you put it together all except say the Parmesan, and then ask for his thoughts if it needs something else like some cheese, would that do it?"

With a little play-acting and a lot of luck, they got the Chief's Cheesy Crusted Potatoes on the menu and it was definitely a hit. Eddie and Charlie kept at this game until they had "helped" the Chief develop nearly twenty new recipes that brightened up the daily menu. The ship's crew helped too by writing comments on the comment cards that the Chief had made up and placed at the end of the mess line. To his surprise, there were a lot of 'attaboys' and even some questions as to why he'd held out these recipes for so long. Ensign Sorrel made sure to share some of the comments with the Captain.

The whole division started trying to improve their part as well. Eddie had told Harris about the overstock of dried fruit and especially dried apples and he responded by making a dried apple pie for the Chief's approval. It too was a hit and put into the recipe card file. Alamillo was a Petty Officer Third Class and had been on the Topeka for over two years. He commented that during that time he'd only seen one attempt at cooking Mexican food and that one was a failure. Without even hesitating, the Chief had him write out a meal plan for a 'Mexican' meal. When he was done, the Chief called Charlie in to help put the recipes together. The biggest hang-up was the tortillas, until Harris showed them how to make tortillas by rolling out the masa harina dough as thin as they wanted and then cutting it into circles with a large can as a 'tortilla cutter'.

The "Alamo Dinner" was a positive hit, with the exception of the refried beans. For some reason, the sailors just didn't like the re-fried beans. The Chief had changed the name of the meal, partly to commemorate the battle at the Alamo, but also because too many people were mis-pronouncing Alamillo's name. Unfortunately, the one thing that made the re-fried beans taste better, the salsa, had been left off the menu. Charlie whipped out a batch of salsa without the benefit if any tomatillos and asked if that were close enough to the real thing. Alamillo gave it his blessing and the last forty or fifty diners gave their approval as well.

They pulled into the port of Naples and Eddie couldn't wait to get ashore. He was tired of the same routine, and of the same meals that consisted of meat and potatoes. For some reason, the cooks on the Topeka weren't big on cooking seafood.

Eddie didn't want to be around sailors and there was one way to avoid them. He found the rail station and asked about different destinations. The railroad went out from Naples in several directions and there was another seaport about an hour's ride to the south. Eddie bought a round-trip ticket and waited. Forty minutes later he was headed south to a place named 'Castellamare something or other'.

When he departed the train, he looked around and didn't see any sailors in sight. So far, so good he thought to himself. He walked toward the sea, hoping to spot a café or restaurant. He passed a couple of taverns and looked but it didn't appear as if they served food. He was almost to the bay when he spotted a restaurant that looked like a family diner kind of place.

When he entered it was obvious this was not one of the tourist spots. There were a couple families sitting at a long table with benches on each side. It was some sort of family get together, as the adults were talking back and forth across the table while a couple of small children played on the floor next to them. Eddie smiled and thought to himself, I've finally found a 'real' Italian family restaurant. He

70

waited to be shown where to sit, but no one came to him, so he sat at a small table off to the side.

He was trying to figure out what was on the chalkboard that he guessed was the menu when the waitress came to his table. In her hand she had a glass of water and a larger glass of red wine as well as the silverware and a napkin. She apparently asked if he wanted to order lunch and pointed to the chalkboard.

Eddie asked politely, "Do you speak English?"

She shook her head no and walked back into the kitchen. She returned with the cook and a young boy. She told them something and the boy asked, "Do you want to eat?"

"Yes," Eddie answered. "But I don't know what the menu says. I don't read Italian."

The boy started naming the items on the menu and none of them sounded like seafood.

"Do you have seafood, fish or clams maybe?" Eddie asked.

The boy turned and talked to the cook and the man smiled and told him something that made him smile too.

"The cook is preparing Zuppa de Mare for the meal this evening if you want. He can be done in about twenty or maybe ten minutes."

Eddie didn't want to be impolite, but he wanted to know what Zuppa de Mare was and he asked the boy to describe it. It took nearly ten minutes with lots of different gestures just to get through the language barriers to find out the ingredients. The boy explained that the 'Zuppa' or soup was different every time depending on what looked good when the cook went to buy the fish and other seafood at the docks. Sometimes it was just fish and clams, other times it had everything in it like today.

He was served a basket of sliced bread, but there wasn't any butter on the table. He tried to ask the waitress, but she just sent the boy to find out what the Americano wanted now. When Eddie explained to the boy about the butter, he went back into the kitchen and brought the old man. Together they were able to convince Eddie that dairy products weren't to be eaten with seafood. It would cause the stomach to be upset the boy said. He then showed Eddie a small bottle of oil and poured some on a side plate and dipped the bread in it. He then gestured that Eddie should try some. He did and forgot all about the butter. This must be the 'extra virgin' olive oil that Charlie was always talking about.

The waitress brought out the Zuppa de Mare and it looked like they'd put everything but a whale in it, there were even the tentacles of a baby squid. When he tasted it, it had a very familiar taste and he tried to place it. About halfway through the bowl, it came to him. This was what he'd had at "Cioppino Charlie's" a bar south of the town where he'd grown up. He smiled and slowly enjoyed the remainder of the bowl. He finished eating the last two pieces of bread with the olive oil on it and drank the last of the wine, except for the tiny bit of sediment at the bottom of the glass. It was definitely home-made wine

When the waitress came to ask if he wanted more, he was tempted, but he was already over full and still had to walk back to the train. He pulled two twenties and a ten from his wallet and asked the waitress to send the boy out to him. She seemed to understand, a minute later the boy was there asking if there was a problem.

"No problem," Eddie said. "I wanted you and the old man to have this," as he handed the boy one of the twenties. "And this is for the waitress," he said handing over a ten. "This is for the excellent meal," and with that he gave the boy the other twenty.

He had almost made it to the door when the old man came running from the back with the bills in his hand and the young boy in tow. He rattled off something and the boy said his grandpapa didn't want all that money and tried to give Eddie the two twenties. Eddie stepped over to the side and sat at the closest table. He gestured for the old man to sit also.

Hoping the boy could translate properly, he said, "This is the first time in months that I have felt comfortable and welcome. This money is the only way I have to repay you for your kindness and hospitality. I know it's more than the meal costs, but when a hungry sailor comes to you and you feed him so generously, you should be rewarded. Please accept this as my way of saying thank you." He then stood and shook the grandpapa's hand and left.

He almost didn't make the train back to Naples, having to run the last block to get on board before they left the station. The other passengers that saw him must have thought him to be touched as he replayed in his mind and out loud the gestures and words he and the boy had exchanged trying to describe the different types of seafood in the Zuppa. He chuckled and smiled most of the way back.

# DIFFERENT PORTS, DIFFERENT PEOPLE

**Chapter Five** – Naples, Part Two

The day following his train ride, Eddie was standing watch in the storage spaces when Charlie the chef came down to see him. He told Eddie that he'd seen the red-headed engineer looking for him so he could give Eddie a little 'payback' for the beating he'd gotten. He said he wasn't worried until Charlie told him there a couple of other guys with him and they were planning on making Eddie tell where he kept the money. Apparently that was how the red-head had gotten these guys to help, by promising them some of Eddie's money. Eddie asked Charlie to contact Ray, the Chaplain's assistant, and have him meet Eddie in the storage spaces.

An hour later Ray showed up, looking very concerned. Charlie had already told Ray what the engineer was planning to do and wanted to know if he should call the master-at arms. The last thing Eddie wanted was to have to explain what he was doing with several thousand dollars in cash. He gave Ray the key to a locker in the cook's compartment that no one had been using. He asked Ray to put the money in a small bag and give it to the Chaplain, but don't tell him what's inside. Ray left to carry out his task and Eddie locked up the storage spaces and by being very careful, made it to the personnel office to see his "friend" there.

Quickly, he laid out the history of him and the engineer and asked how fast he could get the guy transferred, and what it would cost. The personnelman apparently thought he was driving a hard bargain by saying three hundred dollars, but realized he should have asked for more when Eddie said yes right away. Eddie made sure the personnelman understood that he didn't get paid until the engineer was gone.

By being very careful not go through the main passages, Eddie made it back to the storage spaces and locked himself in. He could get out if he absolutely had to by means of another hatch in the bulkhead between the dry storage and the passage outside the refrigerated spaces. He'd seen it open only twice in the time he'd been there, and knew it was locked only on the dry storage side. He felt confident that he could stay down there except for when he had to take a shit. There was a head just one deck above, and it was used mainly by the "rocket men" or missile technicians.

He waited until the cooks were serving dinner to make his way back to the compartment. He knew he'd be safe there because of Joe, the Guamanian. Joe was barely over five feet tall, but about three feet wide and built solid. He never went on liberty, preferring to stay on board. He saved his money and sent most of it home to his wife on Guam. Eddie had seen the butcher knife that Joe kept under his pillow, and had heard that Joe had used it on more than one occasion. Joe snored like a chain saw, but Eddie didn't mind, that way he knew things were okay. It's when the snoring stopped that Eddie would wake up. Joe slept just below Eddie.

He went to sleep that night and slept good. In the early morning he heard the port watch get up to start the day. He just turned over and went back to sleep when they'd left. He wasn't due to get up for at least another two hours and had his little alarm next to his head.

It was the silence that woke him. For some reason Joe had stopped snoring. In the light coming from the opening to the deck above Eddie saw two figures trying to identify who the sleeping figures were in the shadows. He could see the engineer standing at the bottom of the ladder, so the one coming toward his rack had to be one of the hired help. He was about to say something to the guy, but Joe beat him to it.

"What you doing here? You come to take something? You a thief?" Joe asked question after question, not giving the man a chance to answer. He raised the volume so he could be heard by the compartment above. "Call master-at –arms, we got a thief here. Maybe two thieves! Call now!!"

Someone turned on the lights to the compartment and everyone saw who the intruders were. The stewards in the compartment above had the top of the ladder blocked, so there was no way out for the two. They stood there looking guilty until the master-at arms arrived. When he arrived the engineer started telling him about the beating Eddie had given him "for no reason". When Isaacs, the master-at arms, questioned him further the engineer told him it was because he wouldn't pay extra money to Eddie for a payday loan, and the proof is in Eddie's locker. He told Isaacs that there had to be five to ten thousand dollars in that locker. Everyone's curiosity was peaked as they watched Isaacs go through each item in the locker. He found one hundred sixty dollars rolled up in a pair of socks.

By now the engineer was really pissed and started yelling about how Eddie had hit him with a squeegee handle over and over. Isaacs said he'd already looked into the incident at the request of the corpsman and verified that the engineer stated that he hit his head in the engine room and signed the report that way. The other guy with the engineer wanted to sink into the floor when Isaacs started asking him questions as to why he was here. He said he was trying to help a friend, but Isaacs didn't believe him and asked him if it had to do with the supposed money. He kept insisting that it didn't have anything to do with the money; he was just helping a friend.

Isaacs was just about to leave when he noticed Joe sliding something back under his pillow. He asked Joe what it was and Joe just lifted the corner of the pillow so he could see. Isaacs made it a point to hustle both intruders out of the compartment as fast as possible.

Eddie wasn't sure what to say to Joe and the others, so he didn't try. Maybe saying nothing was best anyway. That way there was less to have to explain. He was no longer tired so he decided to go up to the mess deck and get some breakfast. As he sat there he thought about the money and the loans he was doing. He decided that he would find out more about who he was loaning to before he dished out the cash. But there was one other thing bothering him. That "why he needed to make so much money" question that kept gnawing at him.

From the time he could remember there was always a discussion of money in their house. Dad and Mom were teachers and didn't make a lot of money, and with seven brothers Eddie knew they to really stretch their paychecks as much as possible. It seemed like Mom was always at the sewing machine altering clothes to fit the current owner, or putting up jams and jellies. She canned lots and lots of fruit when it was in season, usually picked in the late afternoon when the migrant workers had left the fields. He and his brothers were recruited to pick as much as they could as fast as they could. Often they would go through the tomato fields right after the harvesters had gone through, gleaning the remainder of the fruit, green or ripe. Cucumbers, almonds, walnuts, melons, potatoes, everything that could be eaten would be harvested.

Eddie thought about the times when his parents were growing up and it was in the middle of the Great Depression, a really tough time to be a kid. He himself had a drive to make money. Most of the money he made Dad and Mom would take half saying they'd hold it for him until he needed it for college. He knew they used it to supplement the family income, it was the same thing they told his older brothers, but when it came time for one of them to actually go to college, they claimed they'd lost it. Perhaps they had intentions of paying it back someday, but it never happened. Most of the money was spent on tuition for another course that Dad needed, or for a seminar that Mom wanted to attend.

He was about to get up from breakfast when his friend the personnelman sat down. He told Eddie he'd like to get paid late today so he could send it home to his girl-friend to put in the bank for him. Eddie told him of the incident in his compartment just that morning and said he's not gone yet, so when he's gone he would pay. The personnelman just grinned and said that he'd just finished talking with Isaacs and the two guys that had come to his compartment were having their transfer papers signed this morning. They were to transfer to the supply ship that was headed back to Norfolk, Virginia to begin training for small craft repairs prior to being shipped to Viet Nam. Eddie told him to come to the dry storage spaces before dinner and he could pick up his money.

He went to work that day and sorted and stacked until he was completely drenched in sweat. The whole time he was working, he started laying out the rules or guidelines that he'd use from now on when loaning money. He wouldn't loan money to any married man. He wouldn't lend to any one he didn't know and/or didn't like. He wouldn't loan more than forty dollars to anyone no matter what the reason. It would be harder keeping track of a lot of small loans, but it was easier on his stress level and it helped spread the risk. If he got beat out of forty dollars, it wasn't a tragedy. On any payday he would never loan out more than six hundred dollars. He didn't have a particular reason for the six hundred dollar limit other than it seemed like a manageable amount.

When the personnelman came for his money, Eddie gave it to him and said thanks and went back to work. When he finally quit, he almost didn't make it to the galley before they closed the chow line. He ate his dinner and thought about the engineer, hoping that the guy didn't get shot or killed in Viet Nam. No matter how much Eddie disliked the guy, he really didn't want anything bad to happen to him.

The next day he took all the cash he had except for a thousand and made his way to the local American Express office and had it wired to his Credit Union account in Mayport, Florida. He'd opened the account when they first found out Mayport was to be their home port and had been having fifty dollars deducted from his pay each payday and deposited there. This chunk of cash would definitely help boost the total. Realistically he could deposit his whole paycheck and live off the payday loan interest and the profits from the marijuana he sold.

# POPE PAUL VI

**Chapter One** – Driving to Rome

It was Ray, the Chaplain's assistant, who first suggested that Eddie accompany him and the Chaplain on a trip to Rome to 'meet the Pope'. Eddie thought at first that Ray was kidding him about a trip to Rome, but he soon figured out that Ray was serious. It wasn't going to happen right away, so he had time to plan what to do.

Ray didn't want to stay in a small hotel, but didn't have the funds to afford a nice hotel. Eddie suggested they stay at the Hilton, which Father Fellini readily agreed to but Ray was against. He was not sure what he wanted, so Eddie said he'd pay for the room for the two nights, but Ray was on the hook for his own meals. Ray agreed to that and then they had another problem. Neither of them had a credit card, so they couldn't reserve the room. Father Fellini agreed to put it on his card if Eddie paid him in advance. He said he had faith in his fellow man, up to a point and that point was right at the one dollar mark.

Father Fellini was able to talk the Admiral out of the big car that was available to him while in port. The Admiral told the Father that if he needed a car, he could always use the Captain's. Eddie had been studying his road signs for the drive to Rome, and hopefully with the Father's ability to read Italian, they would get there unscathed. At least that was the plan. Secretly, Eddie was glad that it was the Father who'd had to sign for the car. He really didn't like being made to pay for a new Chevy Impala that he didn't own. He still wasn't sure how he was going to navigate the big Impala in and out of the narrow Italian streets, with dozens of motorcycles and compact cars passing on either side of him. This would be one of those 'learning experiences' that he'd heard of.

They left the pier after it appeared most of the traffic had subsided in the morning. They made a couple of wrong turns and had to backtrack to get to the road they wanted, but soon they were headed to the outskirts of Naples. Like any big city, Naples had some beautiful buildings and structures. And like most big cities, it had some slum areas. The last areas they passed through on their way out of town were very poor and run down. Eddie thought to himself that it could be the poor area of almost any city in the world. Poverty wasn't exclusive to just one geographical area or country.

The highway was in very good shape and though he tried, Eddie couldn't help but speed up in the big Impala. Father Fellini suggested that he keep his speed to about sixty-five and that way they wouldn't get pulled over. He told Eddie that usually the 'polizia' would let you go with a warning, depending on the amount of lire there were behind the license. Eddie thought it sounded very familiar like when he'd been to Tecate, Mexico and gotten stopped. Back then he was younger and not so well versed in the art of negotiating and it cost him a hundred dollars. This time he had a ten dollar bill tucked behind his license, hoping it would be enough. American sailors don't make a lot of money, Mister Polize.

 They stopped just after lunch in a town called Frosinone to get something to eat. Father Fellini was very helpful in deciding what type of restaurant. Eddie parked the Chevy and made sure there was nothing anyone could see looking inside. He was about to go inside to join the other two when he noticed a young man standing nearby. On a hunch, he asked, "Do you speak English?"

 "Yes, signor. I speak Ingles. What do you want?"

 "I want you to guard my car and don't let anyone touch it. You understand?"

 Even though the young man answered yes, Eddie wasn't sure he understood what Eddie wanted him to do. He stepped inside the door and asked Father Fellini to help translate for him. The young man was surprised to see a priest asking him questions and almost didn't answer. Father Fellini explained that Eddie was going to pay him to guard the car to keep anyone from touching it or trying to take anything. When he found out that he was to be paid, he stood a little taller and pushed his chest out, saying something in Italian. Father said something in return and the turned and headed into the restaurant and Eddie followed.

The meal wasn't exceptional, but the service was. There were two people hovering near their table the entire meal, the waiter and a busboy. Eddie would have loved to try the wine, but because he was driving, he didn't think he should take a chance. Ray said it tasted like a pinot noir, which the waiter confirmed. Eddie asked if he could buy a bottle for later that night and the waiter was more than happy to show him the entire wine list. Together the three of them purchased three bottles of wine, the point noir for Eddie and a pinot grigio each for Ray and Father Fellini.

When they were back on the road, the conversation turned to families and it was no surprise that all three of them came from large families. Ray was the oldest in his family with two brothers and four sisters. He sent most of his pay home to the family to help with the bills. Ray's Dad was a laborer and worked when he could, but there never seemed to be enough work to pay all the bills. His Mom cleaned rooms at the local motel which allowed her to get the kids off to school in the morning and then be done in time to be home when they got home. Eddie now understood why Ray was hesitant to go to dinner with him. Eddie liked good food and didn't mind paying for it, but Ray didn't have that kind of budget. Thinking back, Eddie was sorry for some of the things he'd said about Ray being 'cheap'.

Father Fellini was also from a large family, most of whom were grown and married. His youngest brother was still in college and had two more years to go until he'd get his Bachelor's degree. With the exception of the youngest, all of his brothers and sisters were married and raising their families. He'd decided to become a priest when he was about twelve and had never thought of anything else. He said he liked serving God, it made him feel like he was making a difference.

When they questioned him, Eddie wasn't sure what to say. He was the exact 'middle child' in a family of nine. He'd had a sister who was just older than him, but she died of diphtheria when he was two. The rest of the family consisted of all boys. When Father Fellini commented about his poor mother, Eddie laughed and told him he'd rather have his Dad pissed at him than his Mom. He told them of the other boys and what they were like. He told them of the different abilities that each had and how they used those abilities. By the time he had finished talking about his family they were on the edge of Rome. It took all three of them trying to figure out the maps so they could get to the Hilton. They finally made it about an hour after they'd started into the city.

When they got to their room, Eddie was astounded at the size of the two beds. They were both king-sized beds and very comfortable. He almost fell asleep when he laid down to rest. The knock on the door kept him drifting off completely. Father Fellini was there in a jogging suit, telling him that he'd be back in an hour and they'd have dinner then. There were two restaurants in the hotel, one downstairs and also the Garden Room on the roof. They decided that tonight they'd eat indoors because of rain in the forecast.

That evening, at the advice of their resident chef Charlie, Eddie talked the other two into sharing a Chateaubriand with Bearnaise sauce. It was served with a medley of roasted root vegetables with fennel. They started with a classic Ceasar salad and then a soup that could have been cream of tomato but was different with some herbs and a bit of fresh grated cheese. After the main course, they were served a small serving of lemon sorbet. Dessert was a dried fruit compote in a crepe covered with an orange sauce and shaved dark chocolate. They enjoyed the wines they'd bought earlier that day in spite of the glares they got from the waiter. It was probably because they were sitting with the priest that nothing was said. This was one meal Eddie was glad to pay for, but it still wasn't all that expensive.

Eddie ordered an after dinner coffee with a shot of Irish whiskey in it. Father Fellini also ordered and asked Ray to join them. Ray said he wasn't sure what to order and then he remembered something his Dad had said and he ordered a tequila reposada. When asked what it was, Ray told them it was a very high quality tequila that was re-refined and then aged like a whiskey until it was just right. He'd been told about it by his father, but had never tried it because of the cost. Some of the best "Reposada" cost over a hundred dollars a bottle. They sat there drinking their shots, not really talking. Father Fellini told them of their itinerary for the following day and that they would probably be better off leaving the car at the hotel and catching a taxi to the square. They were supposed to be in the courtyard in the Vatican at nine a. m. so they should get there early because they would have to show his invitation and their identification before they could enter. When they all had the times in mind, they went their ways to the rooms.

After months of sleeping above Joe and his chainsaw snoring, Eddie couldn't get to sleep. Ray barely made any sound at all, but finally Eddie nodded off.

90

# POPE PAUL VI

**Chapter Two** – At the Vatican


They arrived on time at the entrance to the Vatican and began by showing the guards the invitation that Father Fellini had received. The first thing Eddie noticed was how big the guards were. They looked like they were "manufactured" to be the same size, six feet six inches tall and weighing about two hundred fifty. The other thing he noticed were their "skirts" and their accessories. They wore a skirt-like kilt that was pure white as were their shirts. The "bag" they carried over the shoulder was dark brown leather and the Uzi machinegun over the other shoulder was gun-metal black and shiny.


When Eddie asked one the guards sitting at the desk if their guns were loaded, the guard just smiled and answered, "Of course." Although he was six feet two inches tall, Eddie felt intimidated by the mere presence of the guards.


When they had finished checking in and showing their identification papers, they were escorted to a large courtyard and told where to stand. They were at the front of the audience, with an unobstructed view of the balcony where the Pope would address the crowd. Father Fellini had made sure that both Ray and Eddie were looking their best before he would allow them to go. Now he was happy the Father had been so particular, he felt good in his dark blue uniform.

It seemed like they stood there forever before the Pope finally appeared, but it was barely thirty minutes from when they'd been escorted in. Eddie looked around behind him and the entire courtyard had been filled with people. The murmuring from the crowd was similar to the buzz from a beehive, an almost monotonous hum. Father Fellini explained that in a moment the Pope would come out to the balcony and address the crowd, usually starting with a prayer.

When two guards came to the balcony, the entire courtyard went silent waiting for the Pope. He came and stood in the balcony and made the sign of the cross. He then raised his scepter and looked upward saying a prayer. He then addressed the crowd in Italian, Father Fellini tried to translate as best he could. The content of his address was about the responsibility of those who have the ability to help the poor. His point was that we are all children of God and that each of us has a duty to give as much as we can to those in need.

It seemed as if the Pope went on forever, but it was actually only twenty minutes. He then gave a blessing to those in the courtyard, and then added those in the Square outside the Vatican. He turned and left the balcony and the crowd in the courtyard began to depart. Eddie thought they would be leaving also, but the guard told them to wait. In a few minutes another guard spoke to the one that was with them and they were escorted through a door into the building. They went up the stairs and were shown into a small chamber where the Pope was seated. Father Fellini and Ray went up and kissed the ring on the Pope's hand. The Pope asked Father Fellini something and he motioned to Eddie to come forward. Eddie wasn't quite sure what he was supposed to do. The Pope spoke to him and this time it was in English.

"Father tells me you're not of our faith, is that true?"

"Yes sir, that's true," he answered. He was surprised at how well the Pope spoke English. There was almost no accent at all.

"But you do believe in God, don't you?"

"Yes your Imminence. I do believe in him." This time he remembered what Father Fellini had said about addressing the Pope.

"Pray every day, my son. In that way God can hear you and see what's in your heart." He turned back to Father Fellini and Ray and Eddie turned and left to stand by the door. The Pope continued his conversation with the Father and a few minutes later Father Fellini knelt before him to receive some sort of blessing. Shortly after that they were escorted out of the chamber and another small group was ushered in.

Their guard spoke decent English but with a thick Austrian accent. He told them that he was instructed to guide them on a tour of the museum. They were surprised because they'd been informed that the museum was closed as was the Sistine Chapel. The guard just showed to the door that they were to enter.

They spent three hours looking at some of the different items in the museum. The solid piece of granite that made up Nero's bath was incredible. At nearly twelve feet across and three and a half feet deep, it was huge. The guard told them that there were four full time attendants that kept the bath ready for Nero at any time of day or night. Eddie couldn't imagine being in a bath that large all by himself and he asked the guard if that were the case with Nero. The guard replied that according to all the historians, Nero never bathed alone. It was also rumored that he slept with no less than three people in his bed.

The largest printed Bible was bigger than the largest bed Eddie had seen and he was asked to point out the smallest Bible, but couldn't. When he was shown where it was, he couldn't believe it. It was smaller than a small box of matches and finely decorated with gold lines. The curator of the museum had placed it just at the end of one the decorative knobs on the big Bible.

They left the Vatican after the lunch hour had passed, so they grabbed something from one of the street vendors. They ate quickly because Father

Fellini had signed them up for a tour of the Catacombs. A taxi got them there just as the tour was starting. The guide was explaining that the Christians were a persecuted people and so they 'hid' their dead in the Catacombs in order that the Emperor's guard wouldn't know how many there were.

Eddie was surprised at how small the spaces were that the bodies were in. The guide explained that in the century when Christianity was first being thought of as a religion the citizens weren't that large. Eddie at six feet two inches would have been considered a giant among these people. He probably would have been highly recruited as a warrior by both sides.

They came to a small room and the guide explained that this was their chapel or meeting room. Most of the ceremonies for the dead were part those of the existing 'gods' and part of the new religion. Because it was so new, they hadn't created the rituals that exist in the churches today. The Holy Roman Catholic Church as it exists now wasn't started yet so there was no right or wrong way to worship.

When they finally finished the tour, all of them were tired and they decided to head back to the Hilton for the evening.

# POPE PAUL VI

**Chapter Three** – Happy Birthday

At the hotel Eddie was tired and decided to lay down and catch a quick nap before dinner time. Ray said he wanted to go and run with Father and that he'd wake Eddie when he got back. He was out in a matter of minutes.

It seemed like he'd only slept for a few minutes when Ray was shaking him to wake him up. Having awakened sailors before, Ray was experienced enough to not be where they could wake up swinging at him. He preferred to grab their ankle or foot and shake that to wake them. He did the same with Eddie.

Eddie washed his face and combed his hair while Ray was changing out of his sweat suit and into his uniform. Ray was explaining to him that Father Fellini had made reservations for the three of them at the Garden Room on the roof. It was supposed to be nice weather that evening, so he thought it would be a nice view of Rome at night.

They were seated right away even though there were several couples waiting. Eddie figured that it was because of Father being a priest. They ordered drinks and looked over the menu, although Eddie knew he wanted some lamb. He'd seen the little card inside the menu advertising lamb chops and that sounded good.

There was a small band playing some soft music and every now and then a waiter would approach them and say something. Then he would hand them a tip and they would play whatever song had been requested. Most of the songs were Italian and although he didn't speak the language, he could guess at what they were about. From what he could tell the band was really quite good.

Their dinner arrived and Eddie wasn't at all disappointed with his choice. The lamb chops were medium rare and very juicy when he cut into them. The one gripe he had about the Navy food was because they had to cook such massive quantities, the quality sometimes suffered. That would be especially true of items like pork chops. The old time cooks had to make sure there was absolutely no pink or reddish color to the inside of the chops. Then they would be stacked up on a sheet pan and stuffed into an oven to 'keep warm' at about three hundred degrees. That was one gripe Eddie had shared with anyone who would listen.

Along with the lamb chops there was a side dish of fennel sautéed with sweet onions and crimini mushrooms. There was also a rice dish or risotto as the waiter called it. His first few bites were a bit tentative, but once he'd tasted it, he finished it very quickly. As he was eating, the waiter brought a bottle of Champagne to the table and uncorked it. He was about to tell the waiter there was a mistake when he saw the smirk on Ray's face. He wasn't sure what was going on until the band started playing "Happy Birthday to You".

He didn't know exactly how Ray had found out when his birthday was, he hadn't told anyone. He looked over at Father Fellini who was grinning from ear to ear. Together they had cooked up this little surprise party and kept it to themselves until they popped the cork. They poured a glass for Eddie and then themselves and were about to toast when a young man approached from the large group that was dining nearby.

He tried to explain in what little English he knew that his grandfather was also celebrating his birthday. Father Fellini interrupted him and in Italian asked what he wanted. The conversation was rapid-fire with Ray and Eddie watching and listening until finally Father broke off and explained that they were all invited to join the party at the large table. The old man whose birthday it was would consider it an honor if they joined in the celebration.

They were made welcome and the old man asked that Eddie be seated by him. Surprisingly, he spoke very good English. He'd learned his first words from some GI's at the end of World War II and had continued learning over the years. Because he was able to speak English, he'd been promoted in his job and had even worked in the United States for two years in New York. He was now a lawyer or as the Italians called it, a consigliare. The people with him were his sons and daughters and some of their children. He asked Eddie where he was from and Eddie told him about the little town he came from. The counselor still wasn't sure where he was talking about until Eddie said it was near San Francisco in California.

When the group heard he was from California, he got the same questions that he was asked before. Did he know any movie stars? Had he been to Hollywood? Had he been in the movies? He tried to answer as many of the questions that he could, but they didn't understand when they heard he'd been in the movies why they didn't know him. He tried to explain about 'extras' on a movie set, but he couldn't quite find the words. Father Fellini joined in and in Italian told them all about how some people are hired to be in the background of the movies, either standing or walking by, etc. It must have satisfied their curiosity because they quit asking questions.

The counselor ordered another round of drinks and the waiter took the order and left, but he stopped briefly at the band. A minute later they were playing "I Left My Heart in San Francisco". And so it went for the remainder of the night. The band alternated between "Happy Birthday" and "I Left My Heart" most of the night, with an occasional other song in between.

They finally said their goodnights and good-byes and Eddie was glad he didn't have far to go to his bed. In the elevator Father Fellini mentioned that the counselor was one of the most influential men in Rome. Eddie wasn't drunk, having taken it slow on the drinks all night. He had seen the counselor doing the same and thought it a good idea at the time.

In the morning, Eddie was very glad he hadn't drank too much the night before. Today they were to drive back to the ship, but by a different route that Father Fellini wanted to use. They were going to go east from Rome and then south among the mountains until they got near Naples. Then they would go west to get into the city and back to the pier. They availed themselves of the breakfast bar in the lobby and then they checked out and loaded up the big Chevrolet.

The trip back to the ship was uneventful, but it was very scenic. The mountains reminded Eddie of the Coast Range in Northern California, but not quite as rugged. They stopped briefly for lunch at a little town along the way and then resumed their journey. They finally got to the pier in the late afternoon and Eddie was surprised that he actually missed the old bucket they called a ship.

When he got to his compartment, Joe told him of a visitor that had been looking for him. He said the visitor wanted to go through Eddie's bunk, but he and the other guys wouldn't let him. Eddie asked Joe if his wife was Catholic and was told yes. Eddie gave him a Saint Christopher medallion on a chain to give to his wife. Eddie had picked up a dozen of them outside the Vatican from one of the street vendors. He didn't tell Joe that. Instead he said that it had been blessed by the Pope, and that he got it to thank him for protecting him from the engineer and his buddy. He was completely surprised when Joe wrapped his arms around him and gave him a big hug. It was the first time he'd seen Joe show any emotion at all.

# THE NAVY I KNEW

These tales are some of what I experienced while serving in the U. S. Navy. The men I served with were a cross-section of the people you'll find here in America. Some were good and some not-so-good, but they all served their country at a time when it wasn't popular to be in the military. Some joined to avoid being drafted into the Army, others because it was a tradition of their family to serve in the Navy. A few people in America 'headed North' to Canada and were called traitors and other names. I can never find fault with anyone who doesn't want to die.

The officers and enlisted men of the Topeka were in a very difficult situation. In the countries touching on the Mediterranean, there were people who loved the Americans and those who despised them. When the sailors went ashore they didn't think of themselves as ambassadors of their country. They were from all different backgrounds and their views weren't always those of the politicians. They were men looking for relaxation and sometimes other unsavory pursuits.

While the good people in a particular country might look down on the sailors for drinking and other pursuits, would they have the same disdain for their own military doing the same things, or would their attitude be different? I think we all have to look inside ourselves and ask why it is so necessary to judge others who have a different outlook?

Like many of the Veterans I have spoken to, I wouldn't go back into the military for a million dollars, but I wouldn't give up those experiences I had for a million either. The Viet Nam Era was the enlightening of the military in ways we have yet to understand. For some it was a period of growing up, while for others it was total disillusion. The atrocities that occurred on both sides shouldn't have happened, but they did. Why? Because the war was fought by real people with different attitudes, beliefs, and values.

To this day, there hasn't been a real outpouring of thanks to those who served and those who died. The people I blame for this are those in the media that had to put their own bias on the news. To find a person in the media who is willing to report the facts is unheard of. Even among themselves there is finger-pointing and name-calling.

We live in one of the greatest countries in the world, with a standard of living that is envied by millions of people. We have the right to disagree with those whose opinion we don't like. We can travel without any restriction. If we don't like those who are in office, we can vote them out.

When you make a statement, voice an opinion, or cast your ballot in an election, please remember that "Freedom isn't free. It cost the life blood of those willing to pay the price."

This is dedicated to those who didn't return.

www.ingramcontent.com/pod-product-compliance
Lightning Source LLC
Chambersburg PA
CBHW071328130626
46556CB00004B/1802